Avalanche!

NATURE'S DISASTERS

Avalanche!

Howard and Margery Facklam

A LUCAS·EVANS BOOK

CRESTWOOD HOUSE
New York
Collier Macmillan Canada
Toronto
Maxwell Macmillan International Publishing Group
New York   Oxford   Singapore   Sydney

To Tom and Nancy
who climbed the mountains

COVER AND PAGE 7: An avalanche roars down a slope in Switzerland.
FRONTIS: An avalanche slide path at Heavenly Valley Ski Resort in Stateline, NE.

PHOTO CREDITS: *Cover*, Swiss Federal Institute for Snow and Avalanche Research; *Frontis*, Jimmy Lawrence/Heavenly Valley Ski Resort; *Page 7*, Swiss Federal Institute for Snow and Avalanche Research; *Page 9*, Jimmy Lawrence/Heavenly Valley Ski Resort; *Page 11*, Buffalo Museum of Science, Bentley Collection; *Page 19*, U.S. Department of Interior, Geologic Survey Library; *Page 20*, John T. Hastings; *Page 22*, Thomas and Nancy Facklam; *Pages 24–25, 26* Swiss Federal Institute for Snow and Avalanche Research; *Page 27*, Thomas and Nancy Facklam; *Pages 28, 30, 31*, Swiss Federal Institute for Snow and Avalanche Research; *Pages 32, 34*, Jimmy Lawrence/Heavenly Valley Ski Resort; *Page 36*, Thomas and Nancy Facklam; *Page 39*, Swiss Federal Institute for Snow and Avalanche Research; *Page 40*, Mill Creek Kennels/Sacketts Harbor, NY; *Page 42*, Swiss Federal Institute for Snow and Avalanche Research.

BOOK DESIGN: Barbara DuPree Knowles   DIAGRAMS: Andrew Edwards

LIBRARY OF CONGRESS CATALOGING-IN-PUBLICATION DATA
Facklam, Howard.
    Avalanche! / by Howard and Margery Facklam.—1st ed.
    p.   cm. — (Nature's disasters)
    SUMMARY: Examines the nature, origins, and dangers of avalanches and discusses preventive and safety measures to be used against them.
    ISBN 0-89686-598-3
    1. Avalanches—Juvenile literature.   [1. Avalanches.]   I. Facklam, Margery.   II. Title.   III. Series.
QC929.A8F33   1991   551.3'07—dc20   90-45622

Crestwood House   Collier Macmillan Canada, Inc.
Macmillan Publishing Company   1200 Eglinton Avenue East
866 Third Avenue   Suite 200
New York, NY 10022   Don Mills, Ontario M3C 3N1
                    First Edition
Printed in the United States of America   10 9 8 7 6 5 4 3 2 1

Contents

Avalanche!

What flies without wings, hits without hands, and sees without eyes? It's the White Dragon—the **avalanche.**

The riddle has been told in Europe since the Middle Ages, when the first mountain dwellers huddled in their huts, helpless against the wild White Dragons that roared down the slopes. Some called it the White Death, sent by demons and witches that rode the rivers of snow.

What does it feel like to be caught by an avalanche? Montgomery Atwater, who was the first snow ranger in the U.S. Forest Service, found out. He was skiing a slope of Lone Pine Gully, in Alta, Utah, one sunny January morning in 1951. It was a year that would be remembered as the Winter of the Bad Snow. A two-day blizzard had dumped 38 inches of snow. Atwater and his partner were checking the slopes for dangerous avalanche conditions before they opened the area to skiers.

Atwater remembers hearing two things—his partner calling, "Watch it!" and the soft, menacing *whoosh* when a thousand tons of snow came down the mountain. "The snow in front of my skis humped up, like a blanket sliding off a tilted table. As a matter of fact, that's what it was, a blanket of snow a quarter of a mile long, two hundred feet wide, and three feet deep." A moment later he was drowning in churning snow. He was somersaulting "like pants in a dryer," smashing against the hard base snow at every turn. "It was like a man swinging a sackful of ice against a rock to break it into smaller pieces," he said. "It was a churning, twisting darkness in which I was wrestled about as if by a million hands."

As he began to black out, Atwater was tossed suddenly to the surface. He spit out a wad of snow and gulped for air. Atwater remembers later thinking, So that's why avalanche victims are always found with their mouths full of snow. You're fighting like a demon, mouth wide open to get more air, and the avalanche stuffs it with snow.

No wonder avalanches are called the White Death.

Those deadly rivers of snow have roared down slopes long before anyone kept records. Some of the earliest reports describe the famous general Hannibal. He crossed the Alps in 218 B.C. in his battle against Roman armies. He lost many thousands of men and many of his war elephants. Some were killed by disease and cold, but most were wiped out by avalanches.

Avalanches have probably killed more soldiers than civilians in dangerous mountain passes. Napoleon's army crossed the Great St. Bernard Pass in the Alps in 1800.

(OPPOSITE PAGE) An avalanche path after a small slab avalanche occurred in Mott Canyon, near Stateline, Nebraska.

Whole squadrons of men were buried under 50 feet of snow. During World War I, more soldiers fighting in the Tyrolean Mountains were killed by avalanches than by bullets—more than 40,000 men lost their lives between 1915 and 1918.

In America, avalanches have caused fewer deaths than in Europe because fewer people live in the mountains. Native Americans stayed clear of dangerous mountain slopes. Nobody knows how many of the first trappers and explorers were killed by the White Death when they moved west. When they didn't show up in the spring, it was said they had "gone under." Prospectors headed for the hills in the great gold rush of 1849. They built their settlements in steep canyons where the precious ore was found. Aspen, Alta and Telluride are some of the mining towns that disappeared under snow.

Today the people most in danger from avalanches are skiers and hikers.

WHAT IS AN AVALANCHE?

The word "avalanche" comes from the French language. It means "descent"—the descent of snow, ice, rocks or masses of earth that rush down slopes. There are three basic kinds of snow avalanches. They are: hard-slab, wet-slab and the airborne, or wind, avalanche, which is sometimes called soft-slab. Each kind depends upon the mixture of some basic ingredients. These are: air temperature, ground temperature, the steepness of the slope, the kind of snow that has fallen and how the snow changes on the ground.

Snow looks so pure, so innocent. How does it become deadly?

It is said that no two snowflakes are exactly alike. Snow falls in different shapes: as crystals, granules or pellets. The crystal flakes are always six-pointed stars in different lacy patterns. Granules and pellets fall as tiny needles, pyramids, plates or bullets. They change after they fall. Scientists say they **metamorphose.** Because of changes in the air temperature and pressure from the snow piling on top, the points of a crystal get smaller. The center grows larger until it has formed a rounded grain of snow. As these six-pointed crystals lose their points, they are pushed together. That's what makes the snow settle. A foot of new-fallen snow can settle down to four inches in a day. At low air temperatures, these changes are slow. All change stops at −40 degrees Fahrenheit.

The shape of the snowflake determines the **stability** of the snow cover. Stable, solid-packed snow doesn't slide easily and cause avalanches. Anyone who has built an igloo or a snowman knows about snow that packs well. But most storms contain mixtures of snow.

No two snow crystals are alike, but they all have a basic six-pointed design.

Crystals make the most solid, stable snow because the six points of the flakes interlock with other crystals. When granules and pellets fall at the same time, they roll over each other, and that's what makes snow loose and unstable. The kind of snow most likely to cause an avalanche is a mixture of different kinds of snowflakes or of different layers of snow. A whole layer of loose snow, for example, can slide over the more solid snow beneath it.

Airborne or Wind Avalanche

January 19, 1951, was a dark, eerie day in the village of Andermatt in Switzerland. More than 18 inches of snow had fallen overnight on top of two feet of snow already on the ground. William Lutz knew how much damage such heavy snow could do. He decided to shovel the snow from the roof of his apartment house to keep it from collapsing. Everyone in town knew how fast an avalanche could roar down the mountain. It had happened before. But the only warning that day was a booming *whoosh* of air racing ahead of a wind avalanche. It shoved Mr. Lutz and the roof 100 feet in 45 seconds! When he dug himself out, all he could see was a mound of snow 30 feet deep burying the apartment house. Although Mr. Lutz survived, his family and five other residents died.

Four more airborne avalanches roared through Andermatt that day. The last one was announced by an enormous crack of thunder before it swept down the mountain. It destroyed an army barracks and pushed several four-ton cannons hundreds of yards from their concrete bases.

The airborne avalanches so common in the Alps are a mixture of granular and crystalline snow. In cold, dry weather, this kind of snow is the loose powder skiers love.

When loose powder snow avalanches, it can be lifted on air and roar down a slope at 200 miles an hour.

But this skiers' delight can be the most dangerous. Loose powder either settles down into "ordinary" snow, or it avalanches. When it avalanches, instead of flowing along the ground, it becomes airborne. Lifted on the air, clouds of this loose snow can roar down slopes at 200 miles an hour or more. Tremendous pressure builds up in front of the snow mass. That blast of air gives it the power that can move four-ton cannons and push roofs off buildings. Survivors always say that the air pressure seemed so great they thought their lungs would burst.

An airborne powder avalanche in 1962 caused the greatest damage to timber ever seen in Switzerland. About 250 acres of 100-year-old trees were knocked down like broken matchsticks. Most were cut off 50 feet above the ground.

Others were uprooted or snapped off at the base. A forest with the tops of its trees broken off is a sure sign that it has been hit by an airborne, or wind, avalanche.

Slab Avalanche

A slab avalanche is made up of old snow. It has been packed down by wind or rain and has settled for a long time. A hard-slab avalanche can start when the top layer of snow breaks up. Chunks as big as a car can shoot down a mountain at 30 to 50 miles an hour. The chunks are so solid that they are still in one piece when they stop.

Sometimes this hard-packed snow is carved by the wind into a wave or cornice of snow. These wave forms are often 30 feet thick and hang 20 feet out over the edge of a cliff. A cornice can be a deadly booby trap to unsuspecting skiers. On the hard surface, skiers may think they are on safe, firm snow; but the weight of just one person is enough to trigger an avalanche. With an echoing click or crack, the **slab** can break loose and smother a skier in seconds.

Wet-slab avalanches are most common on bright, cloudless days in spring, when the snow thaws or mixes with rain. As the bonds holding the snow together loosen, a whole slope can start to slide. A wet-slab avalanche usually creeps along at 5 to 10 miles an hour as it picks up boulders, trees and soil. These pile up into a dirty gray wall of debris where the avalanche stops.

One of the most dangerous conditions is a layer of snow called **depth hoar.** It is also known as sugar snow. In this layer, the large round and cup-shaped crystals act like ball bearings. Any snow on top slides right off. This snow is as treacherous to a skier as it would be to a person trying to walk across a floor covered with marbles. This depth hoar is like a tightly coiled spring. The slightest disturbance—even just the weight of a person or an animal—can trigger an avalanche. If skiers see footprints of an animal in the snow, they may think the snow is safe. Then they find that their weight has set the top layer of snow slipping over the ball-bearing depth hoar layer below.

It was this ball-bearing layer of snow that caused the Winter of Terror in Europe in 1950–1951. The airborne avalanche that hit Mr. Lutz's house in Andermatt occurred when loose powder snow fell on top of a ball-bearing, or depth hoar, layer.

A hard-slab avalanche occurs when the top layer of old, compacted snow breaks up and slides downhill. Each cement-hard chunk can be as big as a car.

In spring, when snow is wet and heavy after rains and thaws, a whole slope can slide in a slow wet-slab avalanche.

Ice Avalanche

In a classification of its own is the glacier, or ice, avalanche. Tips of glaciers constantly break off and fall into oceans or lakes. Because glaciers move so slowly, they are usually predictable and seldom cause much injury or damage. But one of the worst avalanche disasters in history was caused by an ice avalanche in Santa Valley, Peru. Devado de Huascarán is the second highest mountain in the South American Andes. Its ice-capped peak towers four miles high.

On January 10, 1962, a telephone operator in a town far distant from Santa Valley saw a great white cloud rise over

Huascarán. When a thunderous explosion echoed through the valley, she made note of the time. It was 6:13 P.M. A chunk of ice one-half mile long had broken away from the mountain's 180-foot-thick icecap. Four million tons of ice zigzagged down one side of the mountain. It was a mass the size of four Empire State Buildings. It careened from one slope to another. It gouged out dirt, rock and huge boulders as it raced 11 miles in 15 minutes! Seven villages were crushed and buried. One man escaped. He grabbed his horse and galloped away, but most people could only huddle in their houses. No one really knows how many people died. The best guess is 4,000. Most of the victims are entombed forever. They were buried under a million tons of debris one mile wide and 45 feet deep at the base of Huascarán.

No one thought that a disaster so awful could happen again in the same place. But in 1970 it did, and it was six times as deadly. Like the 1962 avalanche, this was also a combination of ice, rock and mud. This time an earthquake shook loose the icecap on the high north peak. Huascarán Mountain collapsed. Thousands of tons of rocks and ice crashed into the glacier-filled basin below. This mass of snow, rock and ice was moving 200 miles an hour. It burst through a narrow gorge like a cork popped from a bottle. Then it surged through the valley, scooping up debris and boulders as big as houses. When it hit the river, it became a mudflow. A survivor said it looked like a wave 50 feet high coming in from an ocean. The people in the town of Yungay ran in all directions. Only 92 made it to safety on the high ground of Cemetery Hill. An estimated 25,000 people died. In less than four minutes the area looked as though two small towns and the large ski-resort town of Yungay had never existed.

LANDSLIDES,
MUD SLIDES AND
ROCK AVALANCHES

The San Gabriel Mountains of Los Angeles, California, are famous for mud slides. Compared to the age of the earth, these mountains are young and still rising. They tower 10,000 feet over Los Angeles. They are 3,000 feet higher than the Rockies. But the San Gabriel Mountains have been battered by earthquakes. They are full of **faults,** or cracks. During a dry season, when fire sweeps through the mountains, the slopes are left bare. Trees and grass are gone. There is nothing to hold the thin layer of soil in place. A heavy rain after a fire can move tons of mud, rock and debris downhill so fast that the flow outruns moving cars.

The average rainfall for Los Angeles is about 15 inches a year. That's half the amount that falls on Chicago. But when it does rain, it seems to come all at once. In January 1969, more rain fell on Los Angeles in nine days than falls on New York City in a year! To divert the water, the city has built 2,000 miles of underground concrete-lined channels. Even so, when the water roars down the slopes, a lot of land, rock and debris come with it.

In 1977 a foot of rain came down in 24 hours. It created a wave of debris 20 feet high. Churning along at 550 feet per minute, a debris flow looks like wet concrete. It's a thick mixture of water and dirt. The dirt ranges in size from grains of sand to cars. Huge trees ride the flow like spears, ripping through anything they pass. That 1977 flow picked up picnic tables, propane tanks, house trailers, a Lincoln Continental and other cars and trucks, plus 13 people who were never found. Debris weighing 600,000 tons filled houses

A mud slide washed away the stairs and walk that led to this house in Oakland, California.

wall to wall, floor to ceiling, or crushed them like plastic cups. In some slides, people have been buried in their beds or crushed against the ceilings of their homes.

Los Angeles has built 120 bowl-shaped pits to catch the debris. The pits look like football stadiums, and some are just about as big. But a **debris basin** that catches all the debris one year may not be big enough for another year's flow. The debris is bulldozed out and trucked away after each fill-up, but the basins can fill up in a few hours. Sometimes they're filling as they are being emptied. So far these basins have trapped about 20 million tons of the mountain. It's getting harder to find places to put the debris each time. Cleanout costs more than $60 million a year.

After heavy rains, rock slides tore away trees and soil, leaving bare some slopes of Giant Mountain in the Adirondack range in New York State.

Geologists say that 300 or 400 of the 10,000 houses in this dangerous zone will be wiped out in ten years. But people keep building on the slopes of the San Gabriel Mountains. They like the cool, clean air, the spectacular views and the privacy. They seem willing to take their chances and pay the price.

Rock avalanches can be triggered by earthquakes or by a sudden drop in temperature. On April 28, 1903, the worst rock avalanche in North America occurred. It hurled 90 million tons of rock down Turtle Mountain in Alberta, Canada. There had been a stretch of warm weather, then a quick cold snap. Water froze in cracks of rock. The ice expanded, and the rocks shattered. People heard the roar

25 miles away. Chunks of rock the size of railroad cars careened downhill at 60 miles an hour. The slide plowed *under* the Oldman River. It carried water and river bottom 400 feet up the opposite side of the valley. When it settled, the rockslide was scattered 65 feet deep over one square mile. It killed 70 people.

HOW DO YOU STOP AN AVALANCHE?

Once it gets going, there's no way to stop an avalanche. But some can be prevented or turned onto another path. Forests are the first line of defense. Trees hold back avalanches like giant snow fences. Mountain people have always known this. Yet they've always needed to cut down trees for fuel and lumber. Tree roots have a shallow hold on the thin layer of topsoil that covers rocky slopes. When a patch of trees is cut, the topsoil in that clearing washes away. This makes it more difficult for new trees to take root.

Forest inspectors were appointed in Switzerland in the 1300s. They saw how these clearings had become open pathways for avalanches. Areas of the forests were set aside as **Bannwalders,** or banned woods. The regulations demanded that citizens "remove nothing, growing or dead, green or withered, lying or standing, small or big, nor remove bark, berries or cones." There were harsh penalties for breaking the rules, sometimes death.

Today the rules about lumbering in the banned woods are still strict, especially in the **breakaway zones.** That's where an avalanche is most likely to start. A dense growth of trees can keep a layer of snow from slipping. But once an avalanche starts, hundreds of thousands of tons of snow and ice, shooting downhill at 200 miles an hour, can snap off the largest trees as though they are twigs. Austria, Italy and Switzerland have active reforestation programs to keep thick forests in these breakaway zones.

It's easy to pass a law ordering people to stop cutting trees. It's easy to replant the Bannwalders. It's much harder to control the man-made pollution that strips the forests. Trees are bathed in acid rain that's carried on winds from industrial centers. The weakened trees fall prey to insect damage and disease. One unusally cold, windy winter can kill off trees that are already clinging to thin layers of topsoil. Winds sweep through the clearings, killing still more trees. With nothing but bare rock left, few plants can grow on the slope. The clearing becomes a permanent avalanche path. Without the natural barrier of trees, the only way to prevent or deflect an avalanche is to build some kind of wall.

Snow fences on the Italian side of Mont Blànc are used to hold back avalanches.

Avalanche breakers are often no more than huge mounds of rock and dirt piled at the bottoms of slopes. There they may turn aside an avalanche and keep it from hitting villages and farms in the valley. Other breakers are V-shaped dirt walls six feet thick and sixteen feet high. The point of the V acts like a wedge. It faces up the slope, where it can split an avalanche in two and force the snow around the barrier. The legs of the V, which are 300 to 400 feet long, can often protect an entire village.

Single walls of dirt, built at a slight angle to an avalanche path, can also deflect the snow into a harmless path. Caught between a river valley that floods in spring and steep slopes that avalanche, mountain people have to build their houses snug against the base of a mountain. They fill their backyards with dirt, level to the roof, so that the snow roaring down the mountain can pass right over the houses.

Some buildings are constructed with one wall, shaped like the prow of a ship, facing a slope. During an avalanche, the wall splits the snow like a wedge. After a church in Davos, Switzerland, was destroyed by an avalanche, it was rebuilt with one wedge-shaped wall. When the church was buried in another avalanche some years later, the snow was so deep that people could get into the church only through the steeple. But the wedge-shaped barrier left the building undamaged. Today such wedges are massive structures of reinforced concrete. They are used mainly to protect cable-car pylons and towers that carry electric and telephone lines.

But for all the attempts to slow, stop or change the path of an avalanche, it is far better to prevent one, if possible. The newest barriers built in breakaway zones above the treeline are made of metal anchored in concrete. Engineers

(OPPOSITE PAGE) A deflecting
barrier protects the village
of Rekingen, Switzerland.

A huge deflection wedge protects Frauenkirsch church in Davos, Switzerland.

study the annual average rainfall, the average wind velocity, and the steepness of slopes. Then they build avalanche snow fences, which are usually 12 feet high. But there is no practical way to build barriers on every slope. That would cost billions of dollars and take years. Even then, no one could guarantee that an avalanche wouldn't someday overrun or outwit a wall.

Snow barriers on the mountain slopes protect the tunnel that runs through Mont Blanc, Switzerland.

A gallery was built in an avalanche path to protect a railway.

Roads and railroad lines winding through mountain passes are protected by **galleries.** These are bridges made of wood, steel and concrete. Galleries allow snow to slide harmlessly over the road or tracks. A cog railroad, winding around hairpin turns on its way to the Matterhorn at Zermatt, Switzerland, passes through many galleries. It is common for travelers to see snow piled several feet thick on top of the gallery, but the track will be clear.

High-Top Research

For many years, all anyone knew about avalanches was learned by watching, by digging out, by helping in rescues, and by stories handed down from generations of mountain people. The first organized scientific study of avalanches began in 1931, when the Swiss Federal Institute for Snow and Avalanche Research was formed. It didn't even have a laboratory until 1936, and that was only a small wooden hut on the Weissfluhjoch Mountain in the Alps. All winter the hut was covered in snow. Scientists wrapped themselves in blankets to keep warm while they worked. Researchers in this new science often had to invent their own equipment as they went along.

In 1946 the Swiss research station's wooden hut was replaced by a modern, three-story building near the top of a series of avalanche slopes. Today all the laboratories use the most up-to-date technology. But one day a small avalanche hit the rear of the building and burst through the back door. Staff members knew that the avalanche, offering itself for research, was also reminding them of its power.

The institute is organized into sections that study how snow forms and changes. Scientists study the relationship between weather and snow conditions that cause avalanches, how avalanches move and might be controlled, the relationship between forests and avalanches, and the effects of pollution on Alpine forests.

At the beginning of World War II, the institute took over avalanche training for the army. It prepared 200 soldiers to protect and guide the Swiss army through the Alps. Each year the institute also trains volunteer observers who collect avalanche information throughout the Alps. Every two years, people from countries all over the world come to the institute to learn the basic science of snow.

Some 97 volunteer observers send weather information to radio stations that give daily avalanche reports. Skiers and hikers can also get up-to-the-minute information in German, French, Italian or English from a telephone hotline. In the United States, the Colorado Information Center was established 17 years ago. It was patterned after the Swiss system, and there are now similar centers in Utah, California, Washington and Alaska.

The Swiss Federal Institute for Snow and Avalanche Research at Davos, Switzerland.

A researcher measures the amount of water in a snow sample taken from the study pit.

Along with the Swiss research station at Davos, three other laboratories study snow and avalanches: Sapporo, Japan; Grenoble, France; and Fort Collins, Colorado.

At War with Avalanches

The Trans-Canada Highway is sometimes called the best-defended highway in North America. But the battle isn't against people; it's against snow. The Canadian army patrols between the towns of Golden and Revelstoke each winter. The soldiers are armed with two 105mm howitzer cannons. They use them to break up snow before it can avalanche. In an average winter, they use 423 rounds of ammunition to guard this 91-mile-long stretch of highway. In a hard winter, like the one of 1971–1972, they used 1,850 rounds. Even so, 129 avalanches buried sections of the highway that year.

Not every slope requires such heavy artillery. In most areas vigilant ski rangers and patrol teams inspect and test ski runs and hiking areas before they are opened to the public. The rangers work in pairs. One tests the snow while the other watches from a safe place. The tester skis back and forth, zigzagging across a slope and bouncing up and down. He or she is always looking for signs of instability, such as cracks or the sudden *whomph* sound of snow settling. If a small avalanche is released, rangers know that one hazard for the skiers has been removed.

Still, no matter how well the patrolling rangers ski, or how much they know about snow conditions, their jobs are dangerous. It's like walking over a mine field. Both testers and watchers carry electronic transceivers in order to keep

Early each morning rangers test this ski slope before it is opened to the public.

in touch. They carry collapsible probe poles in case one is buried under snow. Although they test only small slopes, where there's not much chance of a severe avalanche, rangers take no chances. They always tie themselves to a rope anchored to a tree or a boulder. They do this if they suspect they're getting into dangerous territory.

Large slopes, overhanging cornices and small unstable slopes that didn't avalanche when ski-tested are blown up. Rangers call it shooting the slopes. Explosives are laid by hand, thrown from ski lifts, dropped from helicopters or shot from artillery.

One or two-pound charges of TNT laid by hand are detonated by remote control. Hand blasting works, but it's very slow and dangerous. It's also impossible during blizzard conditions. Just the act of walking or skiing out on a large overhanging cornice to place an explosive can trigger an avalanche.

In the Alps, mortar and cannons have long been used to break up snow before it can avalanche. In the United States, artillery wasn't tried until the 1950s. Then an ancient World War I cannon, called the French 75, blew up a slope. Before it was taken to the ski town of Alta, Utah, the French 75 had been used only to fire ceremonial salutes at the state capitol. But one winter day, when conditions were just right for an avalanche on a slope called High Rustler, the French 75 was wheeled into position and fired. Someone who saw it said, "There was the boom of the shell, then Rustler humped its back and discharged one of the biggest avalanches I ever saw on that slope."

After two years of service at Alta, the French 75 literally fell apart from use. Today 75mm and 105mm recoilless rifles, 75mm howitzers, and the **avalauncher** blow away

This patrolman is holding an armed charge he is going to throw into the avalanche starting zone.

avalanches at most ski resorts. The avalauncher was invented in 1963. It's a cannon powered by compressed nitrogen gas that can hit an object 2,000 yards away.

The avalauncher and other guns are permanently installed on steel-reinforced towers. They are always in position to fire on several slopes. Early in the morning, after a heavy evening snow, avalanche gunners are out knocking down the new snow. After the snow settles, patrols ski the slopes to make sure they are safe for the public. Once the slope has been thoroughly shot and skied, it will not usually avalanche. But any slope still considered dangerous is closed.

WARNING TO SKIERS

Most skiers are happy to wait a few hours while a slope is being tested for safety. Ski-resort rangers are always surprised by the skiers who complain about finding a favorite slope closed. These are the people who ignore posted warnings and head off on unsafe trails. Far too often the impatient skiers are buried in snow. And they are not always amateurs who don't know any better. On April 12, 1964, a group of Olympic skiers was making a film at the ski resort of Saint Moritz in the Swiss Alps. Several of them ignored their guide's warnings and headed down a dangerous slope. Two young ski champions, Barbi Henniberger from Germany and Buddy Werner from the United States, were killed by an avalanche.

The sad fact is that 90 percent of all avalanches are caused by skiers or hikers. More people are learning to ski each year. New sports such as snow surfing and paragliding are luring adventurous people away from marked, safe trails onto untouched slopes of deep snow. And that's where the danger lies. A pamphlet given to skiers in Switzerland warns, "Danger of avalanches means danger of death. There is only one safe way to escape from death by avalanche: An avalanche accident must not be allowed to happen!"

The experts advise skiers and hikers to follow the rules "to the letter":

Know what kinds of weather and snow conditions cause avalanches.

Read and believe the signs! A sign that says CLOSED—DANGER OF AVALANCHE must not be ignored.

Despite all these warnings, some people are still caught by the White Death.

If a slope looks unsafe but must be crossed, skiers and climbers are advised to close their jackets tightly and put on hats and mittens. One handbook says, "All equipment must be loose and free to be thrown away, not only so it will not drag the victim down, but also because loose articles provide clues to the location of the buried person." A knapsack should be carried in the hands so it can be clutched in front of the face to give some breathing space under the snow. It can also be tossed away as a clue to rescuers. Ski pole straps should be taken off wrists, and the runaway straps on skis should be loosened. Both skis and poles give snow tremendous leverage that can twist limbs.

Many skiers and climbers tie a long red cord around their waists that can trail behind them for 30 yards. Usually some part of the cord will stay on the surface as a signal to rescuers if the victim is buried. Others carry beacons, which are small battery-operated transmitters and receivers. Each member of the group keeps his or her beacon turned on to transmit high-frequency beeps that are almost inaudible to the human ear. If one person is buried, the others switch their beacons to receive the signal. It will get louder the closer they come to it.

Experienced mountain cross-country skiers, hikers and rangers carry collapsible shovels for digging out. These can be extended into long probes to poke around in the snow.

Skiers are warned: Don't try to outrun an avalanche. It will catch you. The simplest thing to do is to grab a tree or boulder. Even if you can't hold on for more than a few seconds, that moment of stability can make a difference in how deep you'll be buried. If there's nothing to hang on to, swim. Swimming motions with arms and legs tend to keep the body toward the top of the snow. Don't panic, which is easier to say than to do, of course. But even people who can only remember to push one arm as high as possible overhead and cover their mouths and noses with the other hand increase their chance for rescue. Under the dark cover of snow you can lose your sense of direction. But if you spit, the saliva will run down your chin, and you'll know which way is up.

Search and Rescue

Speed is the key to a successful rescue. Of the 85 skiers buried by avalanches one winter in the Swiss Alps, only 28 were found alive. Twenty-three of those survivors had been buried less than two hours. Rescue statistics in the United States show that only half of the victims survive after being buried more than 30 minutes.

People "lucky" enough to be buried under light, fluffy snow have a chance to survive. They can breathe air trapped around loose snow particles. But that works, of course, only if they haven't inhaled snow and clogged their noses and throats.

A victim buried under three or four feet of heavy, wet snow is almost sure to suffocate. That depth of snow weighs almost a ton. One avalanche survivor who was buried under wet snow remembers that he couldn't even flex his fingers. "It was like being encased in concrete," he said.

Once rescue teams get to the site of the avalanche, they listen for transmitter signals. They look for clues—a glove, a knapsack, an avalanche cord or anything that might show evidence of people. Next they organize a **probe line.** Some 20 or 30 volunteers line up elbow to elbow to advance up a slope. At a signal, each pokes a long pole into the snow in front of his or her left foot. Then the pole is moved to the center of straddled legs and then in front of the right foot. At another signal, the line advances one step and probes again. The rescuers work silently, always listening for a call for help or any muffled sound from beneath the snow.

But even the most advanced electronic aids and the most careful probing cannot match the success of trained dogs.

For centuries St. Bernard dogs have been raised by Augustin monks at their hospice at Great St. Bernard Pass,

(OPPOSITE PAGE) A rescue team in a probe line, searching for victims.

high in the Swiss Alps. In an avalanche, the dogs have the strength and stamina to plow through deep snow with their huge paws. They are also well protected from the freezing winds by their thick coats.

St. Bernards seem to be sensitive to sounds and motion that people cannot hear or feel. Many trainers are certain this "extra sense" helps the dogs feel even faint struggles of avalanche victims under the snow. It has even been said that "a monk and his dog need no compass," because the "Saints" can find their way through foggy mountain passes and blinding snowstorms.

Goodtime Charlie romps with a young St. Bernard, Goodhearted Woman. These huge, gentle dogs are at home in the snow, and famous for their ability to find victims after an avalanche.

An adult male Saint weighs 170 pounds and stands three feet tall at the shoulder. The female is not much smaller. They are trained to work as a team. When the dogs find a lost skier or get the scent of an avalanche victim buried in the snow, they dig the person out, and immediately the female dog lies down next to the victim. She keeps the person warm while the male dog races back to its handler for help. Over the centuries these big, gentle dogs have saved more than 2,000 people. But not one St. Bernard has ever carried a small keg of brandy on its collar. That's a myth, seen only in paintings and cartoons.

The most famous Saint was Barry I, who saved four people a year between 1800 and 1812. Since then, there has always been a dog named Barry at the monks' kennel. The "real" Barry is on display at the Natural History Museum in Bern, Switzerland. There is also a statue in France honoring the brave dog.

Today most search dogs are German shepherds, but some other breeds are also trained for rescue work. With their handlers, the dogs get to the site of the disaster fast by helicopter or snowmobile. Rescuers no longer need a dog with the stamina and size of a St. Bernard. But the real reason Saints are not generally used now may be, as one ranger put it, "Nobody wants a 170-pound Saint in a helicopter."

A dog "sees" with a nose thousands of times more sensitive to odors than ours. It "reads" the ground for information as we'd read a book. A well-trained dog, working by scent, can make a rough search of an avalanche area the size of a football field about eight times as fast as a line of 20 people probing the snow. Avalanche dogs in Switzerland took part in 305 rescues between 1945 and 1972.

They found 45 people alive and 224 dead. They never located 36 other victims. In defense of the dogs, the report says, "The large number of dead recoveries is no reflection on the ability of the dogs; it is proof of the slim chance of survival of a buried victim."

It's easiest for avalanche dogs to find living people, or people who have been dead only a few hours. It's harder for them to sense victims who have been dead longer or who are buried under very deep snow. Exhaust fumes from snowmobiles and helicopters can also make it more difficult for dogs to work.

On almost any winter day there are thousands of skiers on slopes across the United States, and in some areas there

Supporting structures (LEFT) and a breaking dam (RIGHT) were built on Schiahorn Mountain at Davos, Switzerland.

may be a hundred or more skiers crossing major avalanche paths. Most experts say that it's a tribute to avalanche technology and the dedication of rescue teams that so few lives are lost each season.

In the last 20 years an average of 13 deaths a year were caused by avalanches in the United States. That's far fewer than the number of people killed in traffic accidents in a month in many states. During this same period avalanches have caused property damage totaling, on average, about $500,000 per year. In 1988–1989, a year of heavy snows, damage done to roads, buildings and other property cost $2,500,000. Still, this is far less than the damage caused by floods, earthquakes and other natural disasters.

Mountain communities do what they can to protect their property and people from the power of avalanches. But when disaster strikes despite the precautions, most of the residents stay to clean up and rebuild. No one really believes in White Dragons or witches that ride the torrents of snow anymore. Still, there's almost a sense of relief that, once over, the evil disaster won't strike there again.

A pioneer Alpine skier, who knows the speed and terror of an avalanche, said, "Snow is not a wolf in sheep's clothing. It's more like a tiger in lamb's wool."

Some Famous

218 B.C. Switzerland: Hannibal's army crosses the Alps. Most of the 20,000 men lost are buried in avalanches.

1518 Leukerbad, Switzerland: An entire village is destroyed; 61 people die.

1689 Montafor Valley, Austria: Over 300 people are buried under an avalanche.

1800 Great St. Bernard Pass, Switzerland: Several squadrons of Napoleon's army are buried under 50 feet of snow.

1885 Alta, Utah: 16 people are killed in one of the first avalanches recorded in the United States.

1910 Wellington, Washington State: Three trains and a station building are swept by an avalanche over a ledge and into a canyon 150 feet below. Some 96 people die.

1916– Italy: During World War I more than 40,000 Italian and
1918 Austrian troops fighting in mountain passes are buried by avalanches.

1920 Kansu, China: An earthquake triggers a landslide that kills 200,000 people, wiping out entire villages.

1951 Switzerland: Some 649 avalanches damage property and kill 54 people. In the town of Andermatt alone, 20 people die.

1952 Austria: At a ski resort a bus is swept off a road by an airborne avalanche; 24 skiers and the bus driver perish.

1954 Vovarlberg, Austria: An avalanche buries a town at the base of Kirschberg Mountain; 125 people die.

Avalanches and Mud Slides

1962   Switzerland: An airborne avalanche destroys 250 acres of 100-year-old trees.

1962   Mount Huascarán, Peru: A half-mile-long chunk of the mountain's ice cap avalanches, destroying villages and killing 4,000 people.

1965   British Columbia, Canada: A mining camp is hit by an avalanche, killing 27 people.

1970   Mount Huascarán, Peru: An enormous earthquake causes the ice-capped mountain to avalanche. More than 25,000 people are killed by the snow, rockfall and mud slide. Only 92 survive the mass burial of ski resorts and villages.

1972   Obergesteln, Switzerland: 88 people, 400 cattle and 120 buildings are buried under an avalanche in this Rhone Valley town.

1977   Los Angeles, California: A wall of mud 20 feet high strews debris down the San Gabriel Mountains, killing 13 people and sweeping away houses, trees, cars and anything in its path.

1980   Mount St. Helens, Washington State: The eruption of this volcano triggers mudflows and rock avalanches that cover 24 square miles to a depth of 100 feet.

1982   Alpine Meadows, California: An avalanche hits this ski resort, killing 7 people and destroying several buildings.

1990   Iran: An earthquake of 7.7 on the Richter scale causes avalanches and mud slides that bury villages and roads. More than 50,000 people are killed.

Glossary

avalanche A large mass of snow, ice, soil or rock, which detaches from a mountain slope and slides or falls suddenly downward.

avalauncher A cannon, powered by compressed nitrogen, that can hurl a two-pound projectile 2,000 yards. It is used to break up unstable snow, allowing it to avalanche and leaving more stable snow in place.

Bannwalder or **banned woods** An area of woodland in an avalanche zone, which cannot be cut or disturbed because it is a natural barrier to avalanches.

breakaway zone The area where an avalanche is most likely to start or break away.

debris basin A concrete, bowl-shaped pit built on a mountainside to catch debris from mud and rock slides.

depth hoar A layer of snow made up of round or cup-shaped crystals that act like ball bearings, allowing the layer of snow on top to slide off easily. It is also called sugar snow.

fault A crack in a layer of rock, usually caused by an earthquake or other movement in a rock layer.

gallery A wooden, steel or concrete barrier or bridge built in known avalanche paths. A gallery allows cascading snow to pass over highways and railroad tracks.

metamorphose Scientific term to describe the change in snow as it settles.

probe line A line of 20 to 30 people, standing elbow to elbow, who advance up a slope, poking into the snow with long poles in an effort to find victims buried by an avalanche.

slab A layer of snow that breaks loose and avalanches.

stabilized snow A layer of snow that has metamorphosed. It's been packed down so that it will not avalanche. Rangers stabilize a ski run, for example, by blowing up an unstable layer of snow, leaving only packed, safe snow for skiing.

For Further Reading

Atwater, Montgomery. *Avalanche Hunter*. Philadelphia: McRae Smith Co., 1968.

Frazer, Colin. *Avalanche Enigma*. Chicago: Rand McNally and Company, 1966.

Perla, Ronald I. rev. ed. *Avalanche Handbook*. Washington, D.C.: U.S. Government Printing Office, 1978.

INDEX